My wonderful adventure:

Writing this book has been a journey. I could have never completed the journey without the help of friends and family. The journey started with Marc with a "C" and Chris. The next step involved Sharon, Galina, Tanya, Lan, and Arlene. I could not have continued without my cheerleaders, Karen, Bob and Marion, Lynne, Jon, Carolyn, JIL, and my wonderful neighbors. Thanks, Mom, for keeping me on time.

The journey lead me to Karen P. who introduced me to Elyse, who brought me to Mascot Books. Thank you so much for all of your help and encouragement.

- Jo-Anne Dobrick

Whining is Whining in any Language

Story © 2013 by Jo-Anne Shaye Dobrick

Translations by:
Mandarin - Sherry Chen
Russian - Russian Cultural Center
Korean - Professor In Ku Marshall
Hebrew - Ronit Greenstein
Hindi - Sunaina Khanna
Japanese - Chiharu Saito
Vietnamese - Lan Davis
German - Beate Mahious
Arabic - Moshira Hassan

Requests for permission to excerpt or make copies of any part of the work should be submitted online at info@mascotbooks.com or mailed to Mascot Books, 560 Herndon Parkway #120, Herndon, VA 20170.

PRT0613A

Library of Congress Control Number: 2012955273

Printed in the United States

ISBN-13: 9781620862087
ISBN-10: 1620862085

www.mascotbooks.com

Whining is Whining
in any
LANGUAGE

Jo-Anne Shaye Dobrick
Illustrated by Sayantan Halder

I'm hungry.

I'm thirsty.

I'm hot.

I'm tired.

FRENCH

I'm hungry.
J'ai faim.
(jeh fahn)

I'm thirsty.
J'ai soif.
(jeh swoff)

I'm hot.
J'ai chaud.
(jeh show)

I'm tired.
Je suis fatiguée.
(juh swee fah-tee-geh)

SPANISH

I'm hungry.

Tengo hambre.

(tang-goh ahm-brey)

I'm thirsty.

Tengo sed.

(tang-goh sehd)

I'm hot.

Estoy caliente.

(es-toy cah-lee-en-tay)

I'm tired.

Estoy cansada.

(es-toy cahn-sah-dah)

MANDARIN

I'm hungry.

我饿 。

(wo e)

I'm thirsty.

我渴 。

(wo ke)

I'm hot.

我热 。

(wo re)

I'm tired.

我累 。

(wo lei)

RUSSIAN

I'm hungry.
Я голоден.
(yah gahl-wuh-gen)

I'm thirsty.
Я хочу пить.
(yah hi-chew-peets)

I'm hot.
Мне Жарко.
(min-yah var-cuh)

I'm tired.
Я устал.
(yah oo-stow)

KOREAN

I'm hungry.
배가 고파요.
(bae-ga go-pa-yo)

I'm thirsty.
목이 말라요.
(mo-gi mal-la-yo)

I'm hot.
더워요.
(deo-weo-yo)

I'm tired.
피곤해요.
(pi-gon-hae-yo)

HEBREW

I'm hungry.

אֲנִי רָעֵב.

(anee ra-ev)

I'm thirsty.

אֲנִי צָמֵא.

(anee tzah-meh)

I'm hot.

חַם לִי.

(cham lee)

I'm tired.

אֲנִי עָיֵף.

(anee ay-ef)

HINDI

I'm hungry.

मैं भूखा हूँ ।

(main bhookha hoon)

I'm thirsty.

मुझे प्यास लगी है ।

(muzhe pyaas lagi hay)

I'm hot.

मुझे गर्मी लग रही है ।

(muzhe garmi lag rahi hay)

I'm tired.

मैं थक गया हूँ ।

(main thak gaya hoon)

JAPANESE

I'm hungry.
わたしは おなか が すいた。
(watashi wa onaka ga suita)

I'm thirsty.
わたしは のど が かわいた。
(watashi wa nodo ga kawaita)

I'm hot.
わたしは あつい。
(watashi wa atsui)

I'm tired.
わたしは つかれた。
(watashi wa tsukareta)

VIETNAMESE

I'm hungry.
Con rất đói
(toy rat doy)

I'm thirsty.
Con rất khát
(toy rat kaht)

I'm hot.
Con rất nóng
(toy rat nong)

I'm tired.
Con rất mệt mỏi
(toy rat met moy)

GERMAN

I'm hungry.

Ich habe Hunger.

(ick hah-buh hung-ah)

I'm thirsty.

Ich habe Durst.

(ick hah-buh dur-est)

I'm hot.

Mir ist heiß.

(meer ist huh-eyes)

I'm tired.

Ich bin müde.

(ick been moo-duh)

ARABIC

I'm hungry.
أنا جائع

(ana jaa'e)

I'm thirsty.
أنا عطشان

(ana atshaan)

I'm hot.
أنا حار

(ana haar)

I'm tired.
أنا متعب

(ana mot'ab)

SIGN LANGUAGE

I'm tired.

I'm hot.

I'm thirsty.

I'm hungry.

If you really want to get your way, stop whining!

Just say to your mom, "I love you so much, Mom, but I just can't take one more step."

Whining is an international reaction to frustration. When frustration happens, and it happens to all of us, we have choices. We can whine about it, or find another path to get our way.

We are really much more alike than we are different. I hope you enjoy the book, learn about a new language or two, and realize the universality of us all.

        - Jo-Anne Shaye Dobrick
        Acorn Inspired

Have a book idea?
Contact us at:

Mascot Books
560 Herndon Parkway
Suite 120
Herndon, VA 20170

info@mascotbooks.com | www.mascotbooks.com